Shelliky-Booky
——Land——

Shelliky-Booky Land

Louise Garcia

Printed in China

Rev. date: 08/23/2016

To order additional copies of this book, contact:
Xlibris
800-056-3182
www.Xlibrispublishing.co.uk
Orders@Xlibrispublishing.co.uk
734925

Contents

Dedication

This book is dedicated to the memory of Tom and Maura Hannon.

Kitty

Patriot Park, despite the name, was not a park at all. There were no large expanses of green grass upon which to play, no trees to climb, and definitely no swings, slides or roundabouts. Instead there were forty-eight rather gloomy houses which had once been pale grey but were now discoloured from lorry fumes from the main road and the smoke from the forty-eight chimneys.

The houses were built in an even rectangle. In the middle of them, hemmed in by sprawling box honeysuckle hedges, garage doors and the rusting walls of corrugated iron sheds, there was a space. It was irregular in shape. From it there radiated several

1

crooked little paths leading to back doors and garden-gates. It was known, quite inaccurately, as 'the Square'.

Within the uninspiring limits of The Square, Kitty and Niamh and bossy Monica O'Hoolihan played at 'Aunt Polly' and 'Mr. Crocodile' and 'Grandmother's Footsteps'. They skipped over lengths of washing line to nonsensical chants and puzzling songs. Around the time of the Dublin Horse Show they jumped and neighed over cardboard boxes and leaking buckets and piles of scavenged timber in a manner that was intended to be horse-like.

Kitty, Niamh and Monica conducted business in imaginary shops, paraded around in old curtains and table-cloths with scraps of ribbon and braid in their hair for the fashion-model game, and suffered great hardships in shipwrecks, earthquakes and floods.

Sometimes when Mrs. Conway came down to call Niamh in for her tea she caught a glimpse of all three girls running towards the sanctuary of Kitty's shed, their faces strained with apprehension and all three holding hands in a gesture of comradeship. In her free hand Monica had a battered suitcase while Niamh clutched a blue teddy bear. Kitty yelled, 'Quick! Run! It's Matron! She's coming!'

After scampering to safety in Kitty's shed they would re-emerge. 'We're running away from a cruel orphanage!' they chorused in explanation.

Mrs. Conway rolled her eyes and said, 'Ye're gas young wans!' and then Niamh would go in for her tea of rashers or sausages or beans on toast.

However there came a time towards the end of August and the long summer holiday when they tired of running away and playing at film stars. Nobody wanted to 'do' Bonanza, kings and queens or ballerinas. They felt disinclined to conduct any more weddings, having married off half the dogs in the neighbourhood already. Monica's cat, an avid hunter who usually kept them well-supplied with dead mice and sparrows, had left no corpse on the back doorstep, so they could not hold a funeral either.

Monica had developed a rash from eating strawberries sent from her godmother's garden, and was fractious. Niamh, normally a peaceful soul, had spent all her money on ice-pops and as each day grew hotter than the last, was increasingly bad-tempered. After a fierce argument one morning as to who should play Goldilocks in their latest shed-theatre production of 'The Three Bears', Kitty withdrew to her bedroom and considered the issue. The issue, that is, of what to do for the rest of the holidays. It had already been decided that Monica, despite her flaming red hair, was Goldilocks. Niamh had gone in then and not been seen since.

The problem, Kitty mused, was a complicated one. For a start it was too hot. Everybody said Ireland would be the best little country in the world if it only got good weather, but when the heat waves came people weren't used to it. Skinny freckled arms and legs dashing round the Square ripened to lobster-red. Babies chewing Liga biscuits in their push-chairs in the shade got heat rash and wailed. Mothers got headaches and blamed their offspring when they had to make a second trip to town that day for the calamine lotion from Tony Quirke's chemist's shop.

After six weeks of playing there was nothing left to play. Also, they had been in each others' company so constantly for weeks that both Kitty and Niamh were tired of Monica's bossiness. Monica retorted that Niamh was a big baby and Kitty a jellyfish. Reconsidering the matter, Kitty idly wondered what a jellyfish looked like. She would ask her father later and if he did not know he would look it up for her in the set of children's encyclopaedias in the front room.

Both Niamh and Monica had elder brothers who had set off together the day before to go camping in Co. Kerry. How enviously the three girls had waved good-bye at the Conways' gate, before returning to the Square to resume a very dull game of Nine Squares. It was dull because Monica had longer legs than the others so they knew in advance that she always won.

The O'Hoolihans' cousins were at the beach for a week and Mary Crowley had told Niamh she was going to England to see her aunt. Auntie Peg, she said, lived in a palace with gold walls and red carpets, several ponies and butlers, and a poodle named Spot. And so it seemed that everybody else had something to do except them.

As Kitty could do nothing to change the weather, or the fact that everybody else was having a more exciting time than they were, she realised that she must think of a new project to occupy them. She thought hard throughout dinner, and during a walk to Mammy Wrenn's to collect the fresh eggs from the country, but she had no bright ideas. She tentatively asked permission to go on a picnic to the Cross and was told off. She considered swimming in the river, but did not even bother to ask if she could do that, for the answer was assuredly 'no'. Somewhat disheartened, she went up to bed at half past nine and got changed, descended the stairs to brush her teeth and went up again still deep in thought.

It was after she had climbed into bed and tried to sleep that she decided she would open the window. If a cat came in from the flat roof of the extension in the night she would get killed by her mother, but still. She got up, pushed aside the net curtain, and peered out into the dim night. The foothills of the Comeraghs were a comfortable shadow in the distance, speckled with the lights of scattered farms and cottages. Directly opposite her an upstairs light flickered on and a shadow wandered here and there. Curious as ever, Kitty counted the number of windows from the end of the row and tried to think whose window it was.

'Number 16 is at the end and that's the Cahills' house. The next two windows are the O'Flynns, the auld fella wid' the greyhounds is next, and then Mrs. Molly McKenna, so that window belongs to....' She murmured her calculations aloud and then exclaimed in genuine surprise, 'Did y'ever? 'Tis Monica's!'

It seemed strange that it had never struck her that Monica's back bedroom windows faced her own. Once she had said good-bye to her friends in The Square or at the corner on schooldays, they seemed to disappear into their own, different little worlds. She had never been inside either of their houses and would rather wait for them in the Square for half an hour than dare calling for them at their front doors. Monica and Niamh seemed a million miles away when Kitty was sucking iced caramels in front of the television with her own family.

Kitty spotted Niamh's house easily. It was on the side of the park nearest the GAA field, five windows up from the main road. Rather thrilled, Kitty traced patterns on the sill with her finger and wondered what use this discovery of opposite windows could be put to. A few minutes later a wonderful idea struck her. She planned and pondered for a few minutes more and then, having first observed that Monica's light had now been switched off, returned to her bed where she very soon fell asleep.

Next day Kitty pulled on her jeans and T-shirt in a great hurry and gobbled her way through a bowl of cornflakes at record speed, oblivious to Gay Byrne on the radio in the background. Most annoyingly her mother sent her to the shop for tomatoes and an onion. She ran all the way down the road and back, and in her haste dropped one of the tomatoes. Looking around in a guilty fashion, she picked it up and replaced it in its brown paper bag, hoping her mother would overlook the squashy bit.

When she had left the messages on the kitchen table she hurried down to the Square and called her friends' names eagerly. There was no answer, so she crept up the path towards Niamh's house and peered over the wire fence to see if Niamh was in her garden. She was not. Nor indeed was Monica in hers, and much frustrated, Kitty sat down on a worn car tyre that happened to be lying around. She amused herself in waiting by picking brightly-coloured snails off the bush beside her. The black-and-white striped ones looked like mint humbugs. She was arranging her snail collection in an orderly line and trying to prevent an active pink and brown fella from sliding away into the hedge, when Monica finally appeared, followed by Niamh.

'Well!' said Monica briefly in greeting, then her face wrinkled up in a frown. 'Not shelliky-booky racing *again*?'

'I'm not betting,' said Niamh defensively. 'I told ye I've no money and Monica fleeced me the last time. My brother says you get a quarter the odds on an each way place, not a fifth.'

'No, lads,' said Kitty hastily, forestalling an argument. 'Where've ye been? I'm after havin' a grand idea!'

They told her their news while Kitty replaced each shelliky-booky tenderly on a separate leaf. Monica and Niamh had patched up their quarrel earlier on and had both been down the town already with Mrs. Conway, doing the shopping for the dinner. Niamh had tried to interest her mother in a smart red-handled skipping rope laid out in the window of Willie Dee's shop. Monica had received a postcard from a cousin in Ballycotton and she was thinking that if they got an old washtub from somewhere and filled it with water they could play they were at the seaside. There was a heap of builders' sand in her garden too.

'The shelliky-bookys could be winkles,' she said, in an additional flash of inspiration. 'We'll pretend we're picking them off the rocks to cook up for our dinner.'

'Wha's the difference between picking a shelliky-booky off a leaf or off a rock?' Kitty wanted to know, and then, while Monica paused to consider this, 'Listen lads! I've got somethin' important to tell ye. Wait'll I tell ye. Forget the auld beach. This is better. The time has come...' she paused for effect and scrutinised them both with dancing eyes, 'for us to form – a secret society!'

'Why?' asked Monica stupidly.

Kitty sighed. 'Because t'will be some craic, of course. We'll have code-words and secret meetings, and at night, we can send secret messages to each other with torches!'

Niamh looked thrilled. 'How can we do that?' she asked. Kitty pointed out their bedroom windows all in easy view of each other. Monica replied that she had known *that* all along, which only went to show that she wished she had thought of the idea herself.

Their first task, to ensure that the secret society was actually secret, was to persuade the younger kids that no extra bears or toadstools were needed for Goldilocks and everyone was to leave Kitty and co. in peace and not be expecting them to organise games the whole time. The little ones went away mutinous and sulky and were soon happily engaged in chalking rude messages about Kitty, Niamh and Monica on the concrete path.

Meanwhile the big girls had not been so happily employed since the very beginning of the holidays.

Choosing new names and passwords, drawing up the society's rules, copying out Morse code and devising an elaborate vocabulary of whistles and owl hoots occupied them fruitfully till dinner-time.

After dinner they held their first official meeting in Kitty's shed, which they renamed the 'Haunted Barn' to add to the intrigue. They elected Kitty as President, Niamh as Second-In-Command and Monica as Treasurer. After some enjoyable arguments they called themselves the Patrioteers, having rejected Monica's favourite, the Gang of the Black Arrow, as too sinister. Niamh procured a biscuit tin into which Monica, as treasurer, placed three fancy buttons, an old sixpence, a silver-coloured brooch from a Christmas cracker and a Japanese coin with a hole in it. They hid the tin under a tea-chest in the Haunted Barn.

Torch and equipment-hunting took some time. Kitty's torch had no batteries so they 'borrowed' some from Monica's brother's radio. They borrowed

13

his flash-lamp, as Monica did not have one. Despite some intensive practice, Niamh was still unable to wolf-whistle, so while Monica was availing herself of her brother Joe's absence she thought she might as well take his whistle too and lend it to Niamh.

After tea they pooled several biscuits and two pieces of toast from their tea-tables and put them under the tea-chest, for use in an emergency during some as yet obscure adventure. However not long after tea they all suddenly felt very hungry again and were forced to eat their rations. A visiting uncle had given Niamh thirty pence for chips, which they faithfully put in the biscuit tin, but after half an hour they decided that as they had no need for treasure yet, they had much better buy the chips after all. They did, and enjoyed them greatly.

There were no arguments that night about going to bed. All three surprised their mothers by volunteering to go up long before the close-down. They had arranged to contact one another at eleven o'clock and each lay awake in great excitement till that time. At last, the luminous figures of Kitty's digital alarm cube showed that the time for adventure had arrived. She threw back the covers and, seizing her torch in one hand and her dressing-gown in the other, she scampered over to the window.

Feeling extremely daring she flashed her torch on and off two or three times. Disappointingly, nothing happened.

'If they're after fallin' asleep I'll kill them,' muttered Kitty.

She tried again a minute later, and felt a thrill of excitement when an answering beam of light greeted her from Monica's bedroom. Several times the yellow rays winked across Patriot Park, until they were joined by another. Niamh surprised them greatly by flashing red and blue lights. Later they learned that she had found some coloured cellophane and was shining her torch through it.

After a while Kitty hooted tentatively. It sounded very loud in the still air. Monica hooted three times. That meant 'Hullo, I can hear you.' Niamh gave a long and a short blast on Joe's whistle. In her excitement she forgot that this meant 'Danger – stop signalling for five minutes.' However it was all impatient Monica could do to stop winking her flash-lamp for two minutes and very soon she resumed and crossly spelt out the word 'I-d-i-o-t,' to Niamh in Morse code. As she made several mistakes Niamh was none the wiser.

Niamh's accidental danger-signal made everything more exciting and Kitty shivered as she sat on the window-ledge, both from the cold and with apprehension. She wondered what her mother would say if she knew Kitty was not in bed.

They signalled that night for nearly an hour and a half. Kitty tried to wave semaphore messages with her curtain but the others did not have a clue what was going on. They held stilted conversations in Morse and shrieks, hoots and whistles rang across the deserted Square. Kitty began to doubt they were being as secret as the Patrioteers intended, but both Niamh and Monica were convinced they were being incredibly stealthy. Eventually, much elated, they retired to bed, their heads reeling with codes and flashing lights.

Next day, not surprisingly, they all overslept. When Kitty did get up at last, her mother took her shopping, so she had no chance to catch up on the more mysterious of the night's events with her friends. In O'Connell Street her mother popped into an electrical shop. As Kitty waited outside, idly running her eye over the radios, televisions and cassette-players in the window, she spotted something that filled her with glee.

Two long, slim radios lay in a polystyrene box. They were labelled 'Walkie-Talkies. £28' Of course, Kitty did not actually have £28, but the idea was amazing. Perhaps, she speculated, she and Niamh and Monica could build their own walkie-talkies...

That afternoon the Patrioteers met in the Haunted Barn and talked non-stop until tea. The others were thrilled with the midnight messages, and walkie-talkies sounded great craic. In a rare instance of stealing the limelight, it was Niamh who came up with the surprising information that walkie-talkies could be easily constructed from tobacco tins and garden twine.

It was all hands on deck then as the Patrioteers scrambled around their houses and went calling on uncles to procure the requisite number of tobacco tins. When Niamh arrived back with a McChrystal's snuff tin amongst her haul they all sat down on boxes and tyres for a rest and took a generous pinch up each nostril.

In the greenery behind them a black-and-white striped snail poked out its translucent tentacles and traced its slow silver trail across a leaf. Life in shelliky-booky land meandered on.

Mary

Mary pressed her nose against the window of the Sarah Boutique just beyond the shadow of the West Gate. The glass misted up as she breathed on it and she gave it a wipe with a small brown hand. Through her own private circle in the condensation Mary feasted her eyes on her new friend Cecily behind the glass.

Cecily was a dummy. She was such a lovely dummy that when Mary arrived in Clonmel she had given her a name. Mary visited her daily to admire her painted blue eyes, her smiling rosebud mouth and her party dress of midnight blue or, today, emerald green. Cecily was like a goddess, high up in the window of her expensive boutique. Ordinary folk like Mary could only look and long to touch the velvet folds of Cecily's marvellous frocks, as soft as rabbit fur.

Mary decided that Cecily had not always been a dummy. Once she had been a proper little girl. She had lived in a big house with acres of garden and she had her own bedroom that was filled with toys. The Little People became jealous of her good fortune and her beauty. With all the devilment you would expect of them, they had worked a spell that froze her into her present form.

Mary's thought her explanation was a good one. Her mother and aunts said the Little People were well-known to steal human children. They left ugly faerie changelings in their place. Mary thought that from that it was surely but a short step to turning a beautiful child into a dummy.

Luck did not favour the furthering of Mary and Cecily's friendship today, however. Someone inside the boutique caught sight of a scruffy little waif staring into the window. This imposing lady, observing the smears on the glass made by Mary's rubbing, grimly made her way to the inner door. In the small carpeted lobby beyond, a rubber plant lived by itself in a pot, and then there was the stone step down to the street.

Mary did not wait around. She was well-used to being hunted away from almost everywhere. On seeing the lady reach the inner door, she blew a kiss to Cecily and scuttled away. After a brief pause, a second frowning lady with a bucket emerged into the sunshine to clean the window.

Mary crossed the wide street which was still almost empty of people and cars. When she was a safe distance away, she reduced her pace to a slow walk. She was outside a tiny window now that housed a display of toilet rolls and a pile of loose potatoes. Mary gazed idly at the dusty potatoes, remembering Cecily's rich green dress with its cream square yoke and lace edging. Looking in that window at Cecily in her beautiful dress and lace tights was just heaven.

Real life was not so grand. Mary moved away from Murphy's shop, crossed a smaller road and moved on down O'Connell Street. At the entrance to one of the banks Eileen, one of her sisters, was working. Eileen was standing with her back to the stone edifice, holding out a shoe-box lid and imploring the help of passers-by. She raised her big eyes to a young man.

'Just a few pennies?' she whispered pathetically, stretching out the shoe-box lid towards him. The young man eyed her wearily. Begging traveller children were a sight he had encountered many times before.

'What d'ye want to do wid it?' he enquired dryly. He suspected it was to furnish her mother and father with beer and cigarettes but he was interested in her answer. Eileen's eyes were blank and uncomprehending in response. She just looked at him expressionlessly.

'Well?' queried the young man.

'Milk,' whispered Eileen dutifully, her eyes now cast down to the ground. 'Milk for the baby.'

'Go way outta that!' snorted the youth, but he dug two ten pence pieces out of his trouser pocket and placed them on the cardboard lid anyway.

Mary was admiring as she ran up to her sister. Eileen was especially adept at the art of begging. She could always make her face blank at exactly the right time, and look pathetic enough to melt a heart of stone, especially if that heart was female. Men, of course, were a tougher nut to crack.

Eileen hailed her youngest sister, her despondent mask cast away. Her eyes were no longer blank but animated and lively. She grinned and produced 27p from her skirt pocket.

'G'wan,' she said loftily, rattling more coins in her pocket. 'G'wan and buy a few sweets for yourself. Isn't the sun shining and the town full of English and yanks? They goes in there to change their foreign money at the counter and when they comes out they gives me the change. 'Tis only the pound notes they'd be bothered with.'

Mary couldn't believe her luck. She stammered her thanks and examined the handful of coins. Two of the big silver ones with a raised picture of a fish on one side, a little silver one with a bull, and two small coppers. Then a thought crossed her.

'Are ye sure ye can give it to me?' she said anxiously. 'What about when it's time to go back?'

Eileen confidently waved Mary's fears aside. There would be everything their parents could reasonably expect of her and some kept back in secret for herself, Mary and Bridget with all these strangers in town. Foreigners weren't used to traveller children begging. They gave freely. Eileen had no fears going back to the van up the Fethard road with all these ten pence pieces jingling in her pocket.

Mary skipped away happily. After visiting Cecily her regular route took her to Woolworth's. This was a fine big store that sold everything a person could want or dream of, sweets and books and toys included. It also had two doors which made it easier for a child whose presence wasn't wanted to get away fast.

Mary slipped inside and started her explorations by the records, reading the covers and looking at the pictures. The little records played one song each. They were called singles. The big records had lots of songs inside them and they were called LPs. Above the display was a chart which said Top Ten.

'Green Door, Shakin' Stevens,' read Mary. 'Ghost Town, The Specials.' The words on the record covers were not very interesting and often rather meaningless, but Mary was proud of the fact that although she did not go to school all the time like settled children she was pretty well able to read. She liked to practise with the records first and save the best till later.

After spelling out the names of the records on the bottom two shelves of the rack, Mary darted up to the books. After checking to see that nobody was watching she slid behind the book rack into the comparative dark and security it furnished, and started to read. Her favourites were the Ladybird fairy tales. She squatted down more comfortably on the floor and took up 'The Tin Soldier'. When she had read all the words that she could, and had looked with pleasure at all the pictures, she exchanged it for 'The Little Match Girl' and then 'The Ugly Duckling'. She was just returning this to its place with a pleased sigh when a shadow fell across her.

Mary looked up, startled and fearful. A young woman in a checked overall was standing over her with her arms firmly folded. Mary was cornered with no way of escape.

'What are ye doing, ya urchin?' demanded the girl threateningly.

Mary was scared. She would have run for it if she had been able to wriggle away without that woman laying a hand on her but her captor was too close.

'Lookin' at the books,' she murmured.

'The idea is that you buy the books and read them at home,' sneered the shop assistant. 'If you have a home, that is.' As an afterthought she added, 'And always supposin' you can read.'

Mary did not reply. She wanted to say that she did have a home and that she liked it and that she wouldn't want to live in any old stone-walled house anyway. This was not completely true. In the story-dreams she invented for herself she saw herself rescuing Cecily from her enchantment. and going to live with her in her big house and garden.

Mary stayed silent before the shop girl's sneering however and wondered miserably to herself how people always knew. How did they know she lived in a van? Or that her Dad had horses, and her Mam did the washing outside and hung their clothes along the ditch to dry?

Mary was wearing two good shoes with buckles and a patterned coat. Her hair was brushed back neatly in a long, brown pony tail tied with a big bow made from a chiffon scarf. Mam made sure that her face was clean when she left the van. But still the settled people always seemed to know. It puzzled her.

'Now,' ordered the shop assistant nastily, 'you can get outta there and skedaddle altogether. Sitting there mauling our books. Clean people have to read those.' Mary stood up and edged out of her hiding place.

'The cheek of it, reading books without paying,' continued the salesgirl for good measure. Mary felt she could stand it no more.

'Right, Mrs. I want to buy one,' she said defiantly, the sound of her own voice surprising her.

'Buy one!' The salesgirl's face registered pure amazement, but then she recovered her poise. 'None of your cheek, now. Buy one indeed! G'way outta here before I call the Guards!'

Mary grimly stayed standing where she was. 'I want to buy one,' she persisted miserably, half-wishing that she had done as she was told and got going without offering resistance.

'With what?' was the spiteful rejoinder, 'Fairy gold?'

Mary scrutinised the girl's face to see how cross she was. She was afraid of a blow but she didn't think this girl would actually hit her, or if she did, it would only be a light slap. All bark and no bite as her Mam would say.

Slowly and deliberately Mary reached out her hand to the shelf and pulled out a new book with a beautiful cover picture. It was 'Little Red Riding Hood'. The girl was blocking her path towards the counter where you paid, so Mary said, 'Excuse me, please, Mrs. I want to buy this book.'

The salesgirl did not budge. 'Put that back,' she snapped.

'I want to buy it,' repeated Mary, almost as a wail now. She clutched the book to her chest with one hand while the other searched in her anorak pocket for the money that Eileen had given to her. The lining was torn and the two pennies had fallen through. Mary worked them out with her hot little fingers, desperately anxious to show that she had money.

The chink of coins seemed to interest the girl at first but then her expression settled once again into a look of angry suspicion. 'Begged or stolen, I suppose!' she sniffed. 'You bring that money over here to me and don't think you're getting a bag, either.'

Mary stood on tiptoes to place her silver fish coins, her little bull, and the two pennies onto the counter.

'You can keep those,' said the girl, pushing back the two brown ones. 'Or here...' a thought struck her and she gave a spiteful smile. 'I'll put them in the mission box for you, then you'll have some good done this day besides annoying decent people and giving out cheek.'

Mary watched as her two brown pennies slid down the slot of a round tin showing a picture of a young nun, the Little Flower. She could have bought eight Blackjacks with those, or four Blackjacks and four Fruit Salads, or even a Pixie Bar from Ned Ryan's.

He had them in the window and 2p was written on the box.

Mary took her new book and the paper receipt to say she had bought it. She walked out of the door of Woolworth's and set off back towards the bank without looking behind her. The shop girl she knew was standing in the doorway glaring after her.

'What's that? You didn't rob it, did you?' interrogated Eileen sternly as Mary approached.

'No, I bought it. It's mine. It's a book.'

'Ye'll get kilt wasting your money on a book,' said Eileen. Mary walked on. 'And dey'll know I gived ye da money if ye takes it home! Ye'd better say ye robbed it, Mary!' Eileen's anxious voice called after her. 'Or a kind lady gave it ye, dat's wha' ye'll say.'

Mary did not stop. She crossed over and paused outside the Sarah Boutique, to show Cecily her new book. Cecily's blue eyes gazed blankly across at the pub opposite. Mary did not know whether or not she saw and admired the red hooded cape on the front of this, her very own book.

Mary hurried up the street to the giant stone portico of St. Mary's. There was no one in the church but it did not feel empty. Light danced through the rows of votive candles in red and blue glass jars, clustered on stands before the marble altar rails.

Mary slipped across to the statue of St. Theresa in the back corner of the deserted church. 'That's two candles you owes me!' said Mary aloud to the saint, crossing herself. She selected two miniature white candles, lit them from the flame of someone else's candle and secured them in brass holders. One was for her dear departed and one for a miracle, that one day she'd get a dress like Cecily's, green velvet with cream lace round the yoke and at the ends of the sleeves. St. Theresa herself was dressed in a kind of nightgown that old-fashioned nuns wore but she was holding pink and yellow roses against a crucifix in her hands. 'And some of them roses to go with it,' added Mary, closing her eyes again. 'Little ones for me hair and some pinned on at the waistband. They'll be only gorgeous wid' the green.'

The candles threw a flickering light across the wide blue plaster eyes of the saint. As the flames moved the expression in the saint's eyes seemed to change and Mary knew that the little saint had heard and was working away in heaven on her behalf, pleading for the dress and the pink and yellow roses.

It had been a surprising but productive morning and Mary was tired. Here in the church was a dry warm seat, and now some peace and quiet. Mary settled down on the rubber knee rest at the back of a pew to puzzle out her new story. In the cool serenity of the church she was safe. From here no one could turn her away.

Murty

Murty woke up and before his eyelashes could prise themselves apart, a thrill of joy leapt in his heart. The sun shone through the curtains, illuminating the outlines of the twins' bunk beds and posters from Gaelic World magazine blue-tacked to the walls. Murty sprang out of bed feeling elated. Today at last was the day of the All Ireland Semi-Final replay, a red letter hurling Sunday to savour.

There had been no argument the night before about staying up till the little waterfall trickled RTE1 to a close with Amhrán na bhFiann. He had climbed the stairs willingly, every step bringing the great day closer, when Galway would finally sweep Limerick aside and earn the right to defend the Liam McCarthy Cup on September the sixth.

'Isn't it gas how many draws there are?' Mammy had commented after the first Semi was played. 'The GAA are raking in the money. You'd have to wonder do they put the refs up to it.' Daddy had refused to be drawn by this slur on his beloved GAA, nor Murty. In Murty's opinion an All-Ireland semi-final replay was like Christmas coming twice in the one year.

That Sunday morning began like every other Sunday morning. First there was breakfast, people dragging chairs in and out of the kitchen and pulling the table out from under the kitchen window-sill so they could all fit round together. The electric kettle boiled and the electric toaster toasted, and both were carefully unplugged after they had performed their duties. An hour later, after the hunt for Jennifer's earrings and the tearing off of the mass envelope from the little book, they trooped down the garden path in their best clothes.

'The garden's looking well,' said Daddy proudly, hoping for praise. Bright red salvias rose above tidy mounds of blue lobelia and white alyssum on either side of the path. The thick hedges had been sheared with military precision and the oblong of grass was smooth and green.

'Gorgeous,' agreed Mammy, 'and you did a fine job on the gate.' Mammy clicked the latch shut and left it shining in its coat of fresh green paint between pillars painted cream with tan-coloured capstones.

Mammy and little Grainne set a smart pace in front, older sister Jennifer conversed in her most grown-up way with Daddy, Murty came next inspecting his feet in leather shoes instead of their customary runners, and the twins Paudie and Christy brought up the rear.

They all stopped to salute the owner of number twelve who was inspecting his front garden in his vest and trousers held up by braces. Next door to that Mammy and Daddy greeted another neighbour but the children hung back and said nothing. That man was the only curmudgeon in the terrace who refused to return balls that flew over his back hedge. The collection of tennis balls, sliotars and footballs he must have accumulated by now would fill a shop. Murty wondered what he did with them all.

A solitary car passed and disturbed the peace of the sunny morning. The bumper and mirrors flashed silver. It turned right towards the church and Mammy glanced back towards the mental hospital to check the time. They were past the enormous copper beeches in the grounds now though and the clock tower was obscured from view.

Mammy hurried them on anyway and they turned into Cantwell Street. There was no street sign to tell you so but that was what everybody called it. The grey stone wall of the doctor's house towered above them. Murty regarded it with a sense of grievance. A few days earlier he had joined a group of boys trying to rob the fabled apple trees within. He knew every aspect of that wall now, the ferns in the crevices, the creeper like miniature ivy hanging down in swathes. From the footpath the wall seemed to be crowned with an innocuous froth of bright pink flowers but Murty knew there was a wicked line of broken glass set there too.

The boys never had got as far as the apples. The doctor's wife had appeared to hang out the washing and had hunted them. Murty still had the scab on his knee from slithering down the wall when his 'leg-up' made a run for it.

Now they had reached Irishtown. A gang of stray dogs was milling around in the middle of the road. Grainne squealed as a thin, rangy-looking lurcher bounced over to her. 'Get it off, get away!' she screamed. 'He'll ruin me dress, Mammy!' She flapped her rosary beads at it, making it bark and jump in play.

Paudie and Christy were as thrilled as the dog at this diversion. With roars and shouts they drove the stringy mutt back up past Mammy Walsh's shop, to where the rest of the mongrel gang were turning over some litter in the gutter.

Irishtown was thronged with ten o'clock mass-goers. Mammy was saluting people right, left and centre.

'Well, Carmel, how are ya?'

'Great, altogether. Sure nobody has a problem when the sun is shining.'

A few steps on.

'Lovely mornin', Terry.'

'Beautiful, thank God. We'll be going to Clonea after the dinner.'

'Well!' said Mammy to everyone they met.

'Well!' said everyone back.

'There'll be a few missing faces here today,' remarked Daddy, whisking past a man rattling a collecting tin for Sinn Féin the Workers' Party. Murty looked up at him enquiringly.

'People going up to Dublin for the match today went to Mass last night,' Daddy explained.

'Who'd be going to that auld match?' Mammy wanted to know. 'The beach is where they're gone, down to Tramore.'

Mammy loved the beach. Her idea of a perfect summer Sunday was parking on the cliffs at Dunmore East with the car doors open, so that those who insisted on listening to the match on the car radio could do so. But Daddy had promised Murty today that they could watch the big game at Granny's with the uncles.

Arriving at the church portico Murty saw some older boys from round the back of the terrace. They wore bomber jackets and army pants and leant with their arms folded against the great classical pillars. During Mass they would stand at the back of the church. Murty was envious. He thought they were the height of cool.

'Well, Mrs. Murphy,' Mammy was saying in a normal voice as they went up the steps. Her voice dropped to a holier pitch as they passed through the first set of doors and dipped their fingers in the holy water. Murty followed regretfully and trekked down the central aisle to their regular spot. A white marble statue of St. Joseph holding a lily looked down on them all. With the ringing of a bell, Mass began.

Murty's friend P.J. was serving on the altar. Murty made faces at him and tried to make him laugh. P.J. remained composed and solemn as a judge, moving around in a stately fashion with his runners showing under his altar-boy's robe. The rumble of all the people saying the responses was like some primaeval force of nature, like thunder or the start of an avalanche. My dear people, the priest called them.

When they emerged from the vast airy otherness of the church, they all blinked. Their eyes gradually adjusted from the dim light of stained glass and candles to the glorious sunshine outside. Murty saw without surprise that the cool boys had already disappeared. A swarm of chattering people was filling the road en route to invading McDermott's store.

Mammy marshalled her troops, becoming business-like and efficient.

'I'll go into the Griddle with the girls and get the confectionery,' she decided. 'You boys go with Daddy to get the papers. Hurry now or they'll be sold out.' Murty dashed across the road ahead of the others. He was small enough to weave through and overtake the crowd heading for the extra counter set up specially to accommodate the post-Mass rush.

Walking home up Albert Street, supposedly to avoid the crowds in Irishtown descending on eleven o'clock Mass, Murty kept the thick wad tucked under his arm. A treasure-chest of secrets lay locked up in the sports pages, enough to keep him busy all the way till dinner-time.

Back home Murty settled to devour the match previews in the Independent, the Press and the Sunday World with its colour pictures. He studied team line-outs, photographs, interviews with managers and commentators' comments. He read and re-read statistics from the last two clashes between the Tribesmen and the Shannonsiders.

He was old enough to remember both matches in vivid detail. Last year he had been thrilled when Galway beat Limerick in the final to earn their first senior title since 1923. It had impressed upon Murty how a team could come back from a period in the wilderness. Of course, really he wanted Tipp to win everything, but Murty had been lying in his pram the last time the Liam McCarthy came back to Thurles. In the absence of Tipp after the Munster championship final each year, Galway provided the outlet he needed for his hurling enthusiasm in the latter part of the summer.

When they were called into the kitchen for the dinner it was full of good smells and steam from pots on the gas stove. Murty found he was hungry and wolfed down meat and mashed turnip and gravy with onions in it. He peeled and ate four pappies, smothered with butter, and mashed them up with his fork with milk from the jug.

After the dinner there was trifle. Mammy had placed a slice of Swiss roll in the bottom of a little fancy glass dessert dish for each of them, and covered it with layers of tinned fruit cocktail and Ambrosia custard. There was another period of quiet while everyone savoured the trifles.

Finally there was the Sunday treat, the confectionery. Mammy got up to make tea and set the pristine white cardboard box onto the tablecloth. Murty craned forward as she used the bread knife to sever the Sellotape and lift the lid. Perhaps there would be a coffee roll, or even a chocolate one, with a V-shape cut into its top filled with waves and swirls of whipped cream. Maybe seven queen cakes or slices of apple sponge nestled there, or the girls' favourites, fancy meringues sandwiched with cream and chocolate flakes or tinned peaches.

Murty breathed a sigh of longing while the twins and Grainne cried out in delight. Mammy's dash to the Griddle had secured that most delectable of cakes, the square cream sandwich. Its top was golden sprinkled with specks of snowy icing sugar. Mammy divided it up carefully and gave Murty a big slab on a saucer. When he bit into it red jam and fresh cream squelched out from between the feather-light layers of sponge. Everybody praised the cream sandwich. It was magnificent, they said, and Mammy told them again that the man who made it was the best there could be because he had trained on the great ocean liner called the Queen Mary.

Jennifer and Grainne ate their cream sandwich in tiny bits and made it last for ages. They were still sitting at the table licking cream from round their lips when Daddy set off down the garden to pull rhubarb for Granny. The boys complained about being made to help with the wash-up while the girls got off but Mammy called them gannets for eating their cake so fast. She left them with tea towels in their hands while she went upstairs to shut the windows against the depredations of stray cats.

They set off to Granny's with Mammy hooking the key chain over a nail above the letter-box on their way out. Granny's house had two rooms downstairs as well as a kitchen and a bathroom. To the right of the front door was the sitting room that housed the television. To the left was the good room which acted as a Hall of Fame. Nearly every inch of surface in this room was devoted to sports trophies. There was a display cabinet with sliding glass doors and Granny's best tea set that she got on her wedding day was hidden behind statuettes, cups and trophies of every description. Team photographs, some in black and white and some in colour, of club teams and county teams, underage and senior, hung on all four walls and lined up on the mantelpiece.

Today Uncle Ger came to the door. He stood six feet four in his stockinged feet and was built like an ox. He grinned sheepishly and showed them into the sitting room. He was a man of few words unless the talk was of hurling. The television was already on and Murty was relieved to see that the Artane Boys' Band had only just started their parade. Granda occupied the easy chair right in front of it beside the fire, the Independent spread over his knees.

A cheerful babble arose. Mammy and the girls headed to the kitchen for a good gossip with Granny and the aunts. Daddy sat down in the other arm chair and the twins and Uncle Ger squashed onto the two-seater sofa. Murty found himself a comfortable niche by Granda's feet and hoped Mammy would not notice. She told him he'd get square eyes if he sat that close to the television at home. After everyone had exchanged greetings and agreed they were grand, Granda said to Daddy, 'Well, boy, whaddya reckon? Will Limerick bate them this time around?'

And then they dredged through last year's final and the drawn game, but this was not just the papers talking, this was real. The names of Murty's heroes rang out and the highlights of their exploits: the Connolly brothers and Sylvie Linnane, Conneely's string of marvellous saves, poor Fr. Iggy's shoulder.

Murty listened and looked on with blissful satisfaction. He lived for these afternoons with Daddy and Uncle Ger and Granda, watching the big match next door to the roomful of glittering trophies. One day he was determined to follow in the steps of the family legends, and play minor for Tipp like Daddy did, or under twenty-one like his uncles, Ger and Maurice. It was bad luck that Granda had missed out on playing the year Tipp went on to win the All-Ireland. Poor Granda had had to bicycle eight miles to Clonmel after spending the day ploughing. He had arrived worn-out and caked with dust. He had not been selected.

The television was on but everybody was too busy weighing up the merits of the Galway and Limerick teams to look at it until the magical moment came when the sliotar flew in between the four waiting forwards and the game was on. Everyone's eyes snapped to the screen and the only voice to be heard was that of Michael O'Hehir. More alert and attentive than any of them was Murty, the one who not only bore the sacred responsibility of carrying on the family hurling tradition, but who also really, deeply, passionately wanted Galway to win.

Murty willed himself and the Galway forwards into position for every puck out, threw himself alongside the Connollys and Linnane into every tackle and poured all his strength into every clearance with Conneely. The grown-ups had known the sweetness of victory with their own county so were content to see the Galway and Limerick teams with equal dispassion, but Murty was fiercely partisan.

''Tis well that you didn't go up to Croker for the game,' chuckled Granda in answer to Murty's cries of excitement. 'You'da been fleeced. Sure 'tis only one team you're seeing. You should get in for only half the money!'

But Murty was only too aware of a stab of fear every time the sliotar came near the green shirts of Eamonn Cregan or Joe McKenna.

Amidst Murty's cries and the usual protestations about dirty play and the referee's eyesight, Granda was quietly teaching Murty.

'See that, boy? What happened there?'

'Why shouldn't he have gone for goal, Murty?'

'Was yer man inside the parallelogram or out of it?'

'Is it a 65 or a penalty?'

It was hard for Murty to answer questions and follow the game while simultaneously channelling every spark and mote of his energy into willing Galway to succeed. In the heat of the action, time seemed hardly to exist anymore. All of a sudden, to Murty's surprise, the ref blew a long blast on his whistle.

'What's he blowing now for?' he asked indignantly, but the players trooping off the pitch to the dressing rooms gave him his answer. Murty couldn't believe it was half-time already. It seemed seconds since the ball had been thrown in at the start.

Granny must have had a better sense of timing than Murty though because right on cue she appeared from the kitchen, dressed in her blue wrap-around apron and carrying a tray of tea and sweet biscuits. For Murty and the twins there was a can of 7Up to share, a great treat.

'Bless you, pet,' said Granda, scooping his mug off the tray gratefully. They heard Granny relaying the score to the group in the kitchen but the news was quickly eclipsed by the topic of the style to be had at Dunnes' sale, even before the kitchen door had closed again.

The advertisements for cattle remedies and Barry's tea in the break took a surprisingly long time. Murty could remember drinking his 7Up and nibbling his way through two biscuits quite clearly afterwards. The second half of the game however passed itself out in seconds, or so it seemed to Murty. One minute the players emerged back onto the pitch, the next there was a fierce crack as hurleys clashed, and then it was non-stop puck-outs and 65s, tackles and solo runs, the scores notching up in the corner of the screen and the maroon and green-clad figures a blur across the field. Green and white flags waved at either end of the field, linesmen and managers paced, the little white ball swooped and arched through the sky and almost as quickly as it had begun it was over.

Horrified, Murty felt a pricking sensation behind his eyelids. It felt like he was going to cry! If Galway had lost it would have been shameful enough, but considering his team had actually won, it was quite inexplicable! Murty ran out through the kitchen to the bathroom and when he came back he felt perfectly normal again.

'So what did you think of the match, Murty?' Mammy asked later that night. They were sitting in the sitting room with the sofa pulled close to the fire.

Grainne had already been sent up to bed and the twins could be heard messing in the bathroom, supposedly cleaning their teeth.

'I don't know, Mammy,' replied Murty quite honestly, 'It all happened so fast and it was so exciting, it's like I didn't see it at all.' He looked at her anxiously, trying to gauge her mood and then burst out:

'Please Mammy, oh, pl-ease Mammy, if I promise to be good forever, cross my heart and hope to die... will y'ever let me stay up late tonight to watch the Sunday Game?'

Nonie

Friday afternoon in school is a hard time to concentrate. Some of the girls in Fourth Class were day-dreaming or thinking about the walk home to two days of freedom when Sister Assumpta said what they would be doing in English on Monday morning.

'News,' said the nun, 'is not just what is in the papers. Didn't the angel Gabriel bring good news to Our Lady?'

Those who were listening nodded, and murmured, 'Yes, Sister.' Sister Assumpta's sharp eyes raked the room and spotted those who had not answered or were gazing out of the window. With a rap of the leather strap on her desk she recalled their attention.

'You may receive news in a letter or perhaps if you have one, by a telephone, or from a neighbour. On Monday I want each of you to come prepared to give us some news, something of interest that has happened to you between now and then. When we have heard news from everyone, each girl will write her news down in her copy book. Are there any questions?'

Mena, a gloomy child wearing spectacles, put up her right hand. 'Does it have to be good news, Sister?'

'No,' said Sister Assumpta with a bite of irritation in her voice, 'but I think we'd rather hear something positive and interesting if at *all* possible, Mena.'

The bell rang shortly after that and the class was dismissed, with a last reminder about having to attend Mass on Sunday morning. Nonie Morrison walked home with two friends who lived in the same corporation housing development as she did.

'How will we know what news to give her?' asked Dolores.

'How will ya know till it happens, ya stupid-lookin' eejit?' asked Grainne in reply. 'That's why 'tis called news, 'cos 'tis new. You don't know what 'tis till 'tis after happening.'

They said their good-byes and turned in through their own metal gates. Nonie ran up the path and stuck her hand inside the letter-box reaching for the key chain. Some people left their front doors open when the weather was fine, but Mammy said times were changing and you had to be careful. The Morrisons all used the key on the chain to let themselves in. At night time it was pulled up out of reach and looped over a nail on the inside above the letter box.

Nonie blessed herself automatically as she passed the holy water font and ran in to find Mammy. 'We've to get interesting news for Sister for Monday,' she informed her. 'Can we do something exciting tomorrow, Mammy?'

'We can of course, pet,' said Mammy absent-mindedly. She was balancing clothes on the bathroom scales on the kitchen floor, preparing a load for the new washing machine. They had never had one before and Mammy studied the instruction book carefully every time she used it. She said she was afraid of her life of doing damage to the wonderful machine.

'Take off that uniform now and leave it here with me, and put on a pants and a gansey and go out and play till yer tea is ready. Maybe we'll take a walk out to St. Patrick's Well tomorrow if the day is fine. Would that be good enough, d'you think?'

At the time Nonie was doubtful but when they returned from the Well the next evening she doubted no longer. Indeed, she looked flushed and full of suppressed excitement, so much so that Mammy asked her why she was looking so pleased with herself. Nonie said nothing but kept grinning in a maddening way. Two of her brothers and sisters, Mickey and Regina, piled on top of her, tickling and pinching her to make her say what was so funny, but still Nonie would tell no one what had happened to make her look, as Daddy put it, like a pup with two tails. It was most mysterious.

In bed that night Nonie hugged her battered teddy bear. Only he should know the secret.

'D'ye know how I'd be always wanting Sunday to last forever and Monday comes too soon?' she asked him. 'Well tonight I'm just waiting till Monday comes and Sunday is only a big nuisance getting in the way. D'ye want to know why?' The bear obviously did, because Nonie proceeded to whisper in a voice full of awed importance. 'I've the best piece of news Sister Assumpta will ever have heard in her whole life. There's nobody will have news like mine. I'm telling ye now, t'will be some stir when I tell my news on Monday.'

Nonie thought Sunday had never been so long. Through all of it her mind kept returning to one obsession – telling her marvellous news to the class on Monday morning.

Finally Monday dawned. Mammy had a jug of raw milk from Michael Cullinane. He still drove round the town on a horse-drawn cart with his churns on the back. Mammy skimmed off the cream and Nonie, Regina, Mickey and the rest put it on their porridge with golden syrup. After the breakfast Nonie hurried to get ready to go to school. She put on her hand-knitted cardigan and her hand-me-down coat over her shirt, tie and pinafore and ran out the back way to meet Dolores and Grainne. They all walked to school together.

Dolores had remembered about the English lesson too and she was most excited. She had thrilling news, she said. A frown wrinkled Nonie's brow. Surely Dolores' news could not outshine her own? Her fears were soon allayed however.

'Yes, and we spent the whole evening in Dungarvan from half past two till six,' Dolores was saying impressively. 'On the way down we stopped at the grotto at Ballymacarberry. We saw the monument to Master McGrath too, and my cousin had a racing bike and I got a spin on it. T'was some day!'

Nonie agreed that Dolores' long, treat-laden trip to her aunt's was good, but privately she felt sure her own news would cause more excitement. After prayers they sang a hymn and marched back to their classroom. Nonie's favourite nun, Sister Dymphna, was playing the piano. Wisps of her fly-away hair were escaping from the white band round her head. Her lively brown eyes twinkled under her humorous-looking eyebrows. As Nonie marched past the nun smiled at her good-naturedly.

Next there was roll-call and some Irish exercises and then at last Sister Assumpta said it was time to give their news. Nonie fidgeted in her seat, waiting for her turn.

'Ciúineas!' said Sr. Assumpta. 'What have you for us, Clodagh?'

'Me cat had kittens, Sister,' announced Clodagh proudly.

'My cat,' corrected Sister.

'No, t'was mine,' disagreed Clodagh.

This misunderstanding did not improve Sr. Assumpta's mood. She frowned and her hand twitched towards the strap on the desk but she continued in a warning tone, 'And what were these kittens like, Clodagh?'

'There was wan black and two brackety fellas and wan little fella white wid' black ears and a moustache.' For some reason this made Nonie and some of the other girls giggle. Men had moustaches, not kittens. Sister however was not amused by the reaction.

'Good, Clodagh,' she said, but her eyes were scanning desks to see who was giggling.

Clodagh was enjoying the sense of popularity that came from making the class laugh. 'Oh,' she put in hurriedly, 'and we called the little fella with the moustache Charlie Chaplin.'

At this there were actual shouts of laughter and Sister's face grew dark. The leather hit the desk as she restored order.

'Thank you, Clodagh, that will be all,' she said repressively. 'Now, Colette. What can you tell us please?'

'I had to go up to St. Joseph's wid' me brudder and he got five stiitches in his leg, Sister,' reported Colette. Sister's interrogation revealed that the brother had become tangled in an old bedstead and barbed wire in a neighbour's hedge.

This story also caused some amusement and Sister Assumpta remarked caustically that she was not training comedians. She did not think that giddiness should be encouraged at any time, but certainly not on a Monday morning. She deliberately picked on the most earnest members of the class next. They managed to convey their news without raising a titter.

Mary-Lou's sister had come home from England. Breda Flannery had a new doll and Breda Cashman a new baby brother. Sister's good humour was restored by these respectful contributions and she thawed as she said, 'Well now, sure there's been great excitement all round this weekend.'

At last it was Nonie's turn. Sister knew Nonie's mother and generally found Nonie a willing and able pupil. She was as amiable as a nun with a reputation for being cross could ever be when she asked, 'So now, Nonie. What happened ye this weekend?'

Nonie gasped and took a deep breath. Her moment had come at last. She was bursting to tell. 'Please, Sister,' she said, red-faced with suppressed excitement, 'I saw a leprechaun.' Then she beamed round at everybody. Most of the girls looked incredulous and some began to laugh, not just giggle, but really laugh out loud.

'Nonie Morrison,' snapped Sister Assumpta. 'I asked you a civil question. Kindly answer it without making yourself out for an amadán.'

'I did answer, Sister,' returned Nonie, surprised. 'I said I saw a leprechaun.'

'There's a difference between telling stories and giving news and I do not approve of story-tellers. Dolores! Your news please? Nonie has none.'

After all the build-up to the great moment, Nonie did not now have the sense to stay quiet.

'I have news! I have!' she cried out wildly. 'I saw a leprechaun! Wasn't he over at St. Patrick's Well with a red jersey on him!'

Sister Assumpta glared at Nonie with her eyebrows nearly meeting in the middle. She leaned low over the desk gripping its edges but still she towered over the girls in the front row. 'Nonie Morrison. Let me tell you what happens to wicked girls who persist in telling stories. One day they look into the mirror and what do they see? They see that their tongue is shrivelled and turned black as coal,' she said in a terrible voice. The class fell silent.

Nonie was close to tears. 'I'm not telling stories,' she wailed desperately. 'I saw a real leprechaun and he was whistling on a piece of marsh grass. After I saw him doing it he disappeared but I picked the exact same grass that was growing there in the mud and I blew into it and it made a squeak like his...' But Sister Assumpta cut the girl short.

'Nonie Morrison, leave the room,' she ordered. 'I'll not have storytellers in my classroom.' There were no giggles to be heard now. The room was deathly quiet. To be sent out of the room was in some ways worse than being hit on the hand because it so rarely happened. People said that if the Principal came past and saw a girl standing outside a classroom that girl would be expelled, there and then.

To everyone's amazement Nonie did not move. 'No, no,' she pleaded, 'I did see him, I did. I've been waiting all yesterday to tell about it. T'was as real as you standing there.'

Sister Assumpta left her position between the blackboard and the desk and threaded her way through two lines of desks towards Nonie.

'I can see I will have to escort you from the room,' she said in a voice of controlled fury. Before the nun's grip could close upon her upper arm, Nonie had sprung from her desk and stumbled to the door. She could hardly see where she was going as tears clouded her vision. As she reached the classroom door they started to carve a hot path down her cheeks. 'I did see a leprechaun, I seen him, I did!' she sobbed, wrenching open the door and passing through it. In her misery she shut it too fast and it banged loudly but, thank goodness, Sister Assumpta did not re-appear even more terrible than before.

Nonie leant against the corridor wall. Everything looked hazy through her tears. 'They think I tell stories an' I don't,' she stammered aloud to herself. 'I did see a leprechaun, I did!' She began to sob and slid down the wall until she was sitting on the floor, her head in her arms, crying piteously.

'I saw one too once,' said a reflective voice nearby. Nonie stopped sobbing in amazement. She raised her tear-stained face to see who had spoken. Sister Dymphna, the music nun, had been pinning up a notice on a board. She smiled welcomingly.

'Oh yes,' she said gently. 'When I was quite a little girl I saw a leprechaun and nobody believed me either.'

Nonie gaped. 'You did?'

'I did,' said Sister Dymphna cheerfully. 'I remember I was staying at my grandfather's and we went up to the Cross on August bank holiday Monday. T'was quite a new thing back then. When the Mass was finished we two went down a different path to the crowd and we arrived at an auld place my grandfather knew. T'was in the Ragwell that I saw the leprechaun.'

Nonie rubbed away a tear and gazed at Sister Dymphna. 'Was he.... was he about this tall?' she whispered, indicating with a small hand a height eighteen inches from the ground.

'He was indeed,' smiled Sister Dymphna. 'About a foot and a half tall, I'd say. I wanted to know had he a pot of gold or did he leave it under a rainbow somewhere but he was off as soon as he saw me peeping at him through the leaves of the whitethorn tree.'

'My leprechaun was whistling music through a hollow grass,' ventured Nonie. 'T'was the music led me to him. No one else heard it at all.'

Sister Dymphna nodded wisely. 'There's a blessing,' she said, 'hearing the sidhe music. Where was this wee fella, anyway?'

'Up at St. Patrick's Well,' replied Nonie eagerly. 'Out past Jackson's Cross and the new houses and the field of straw bales. Or else you can go the Marlfield way, up past the ice-cream shop in the village.'

'Well now,' said Sister Dymphna. 'I must pay a visit myself and see will he show himself to me. They do like the holy wells and the whitethorn trees.'

Nonie nodded happily. Sister Dymphna was so kind and understanding, and imagine! She too had seen a little person when she was small! Temporarily Nonie had quite forgotten about the wrath of Sister Assumpta.

At that moment however the bell rang for small break. There was a clatter of desks and chairs and Clodagh and Mary-Lou ran out. They cast curious glances at Nonie as they passed and Nonie heard them giggle at her as they turned the corner at the end of the passage. She got up from her position on the floor and wondered miserably what Sister Assumpta would say. Sister Dymphna smiled reassuringly.

Sister Assumpta sailed out of the classroom and pounced upon Nonie. 'Nonie Morrison,' she said in a sad voice. 'You are to be pitied for you'll never amount to anything. I don't want to hear another word of your ridiculous story when you rejoin my class. While the others are writing their news you will copy out one hundred times this proverb: 'An honest man does not make himself a dog for the sake of a bone.' I shall check your lines tomorrow at roll call. Now go on outside with the others.'

Nonie looked with a mixture of relief and anger at Sister Assumpta's back as it marched away. Sister Dymphna, still hovering by the notice-board, caught her attention again.

'Would you mind if I gave you a small bit of advice, Nonie?' she asked. 'If I were you I'd keep the leprechaun to myself. People who have never seen one can behave strangely to people who have. Don't the Little People prefer not to be talked about anyway? T'was a privilege to hear and see him, but t'was only for your ears and eyes, a secret between the two of ye.' Sister Dymphna smiled her dimpled smile and Nonie smiled back. Then the little nun bustled off up the corridor and Nonie went out to the playground, wiping her eyes and face on the sleeves of her cardigan as she did so.

Feeling much more cheerful, Nonie cast her mind forwards to next weekend. If Daddy didn't have a match to go to and Mammy didn't have relations visiting and if the evening was fine on Saturday or Sunday, then maybe one of them would take her out to St. Patrick's Well again. She would circle the lake three times as she had done before, and drink the holy water from the tin cup on a chain. Then while Mickey and Regina were climbing into the stone circle where the water bubbled up, or into the window nooks of the old church, she would go slowly to the wall and look across the next field to the big grey rock under the whitethorn tree.

Maybe the strains of the haunting music would float across to her again? Maybe she would see him with the grass stem pipe between his long fingers, poised to sound a note. His jewel-bright eyes would look up at hers, just for a moment.

Then he would dive and be gone like a streak of light, disappearing between the leaves of the tall yellow flags. The wind would ruffle the surface of the lake, fragmenting the reflection of the great stone cross, and a musical whispering would rise from the flags and rushes. Nonie would know, and be quite, quite sure, that here was more than the voice of the wind.

Finbarr

Finbarr was tall for his age, and strong, and consequently something of a local hero on the sports field. The Nationalist reports on underage hurling and football commended him. Opposing teams groaned when they saw him togging out and called him a 'skyscraper'. You could find his name in the lists in the handball alley and when badminton sessions occurred in the GAA centre hall, Finbarr was sure to be there too.

Finbarr called every day for his nearest pals, Jimmy and Peadar, and the three of them plus assorted younger hangers-on pucked, kicked and hit tennis balls up and down the street for hours on end.

Grown-ups on the street rejoiced when Jimmy got a present of a cheap badminton set from Woolworth's.

'At least an innocent body passing with their messages won't be too badly harmed if 'tis only a shuttlecock gone astray,' said Mrs. Delaney. 'I got an awful belt of some class of a ball one day.'

''Tis good news for himself's dahlias too,' agreed Mrs. Lynch, from the other side of the hedge. 'He's tormented with balls coming into the garden.'

One of the great things about being a keen sportsman was that it gave a fella more excuses to wander away from the home turf. Finbarr, Jimmy and Peadar had permission to play pitch and putt in the grounds of the mental hospital, and to go down to the GAA field whenever there was a match. The black and white fingerpost next to the hospital wall provided a handy short-cut for the lads, as well as directions to lorry drivers heading for Limerick or Waterford. Scaling the wall of the GAA field was harder, but not impossible, if you knew the two weak spots where the barbed wire was broken. Finbarr knew them both well. He and the lads spent many happy hours reliving the Sunday Game in the goalmouth, providing their own commentary in the style of Michael O'Hehir.

It was rare enough in Finbarr's street to look for playmates and find no one eager for a game of something, but the one large shed door that was flat and not corrugated provided a substitute player when the street was deserted. When Jimmy was down town with his mother and Peadar helping deliver coal with his uncle, Finbarr's imagined companions peopled the alley and practised alongside him. There was Christy Ring showing him what ambidexterity meant and the Rackards, who were well-known for their barn door training sessions. Even Jimmy Connors put in an appearance now and again when Finbarr could get a loan of his sister Marion's tennis racket.

There was only one flaw to the rhythm of the long summer holiday as far as Finbarr was concerned, and that was the lure of the river, a spell from which no boy but he seemed to escape. He didn't mind going up the Green fishing, with a rod fitted with a bobble and worm. He might even risk trying for eels from one of the good casting spots along the quay. None of the boys were supposed to go to the Green or the quay or anywhere near the perils of the river, but so long as no neighbour saw them and got talking to the mothers they could get away with it. No, Finbarr's big problem came when the weather turned really hot.

'There's a big 'H' coming in over Ireland,' announced his mother one evening in August after peering closely at the RTE weather maps after the nine o'clock news.

'Wha'?' said Finbarr.

'A big 'H'. When you see a big 'H' heading in from the Atlantic it means the weather will be beautiful.'

'High pressure,' said his father, rousing himself from the Evening Herald. 'Tha's what it stands for.'

'And when you see the big 'L' coming it means nothing only rain,' added his sister Marion, bringing in the post-news tray laden with mugs of tea and a package of biscuits.

Sure enough next day, when Finbarr looked out across the corrugated shed roofs and the lines of crows perched on the ESB wires, there was not a cloud in the sky. By dinner time all the lads were agreeing that the sun was splitting the rocks. The girls, who had been playing at the other end of the street, seemed to agree.

'Look at yer wan,' hissed Jimmy, pointing. Two of the girls had gone inside and re-appeared wearing shorts and a mini-skirt.

'Scandalous,' agreed Peadar. 'Sure yer wan from England is very bould.'

The boys adjusted to the weather without causing such a sensation. Finbarr tied his sweater round his waist over his jeans. Jimmy took his runners off and said he was Babs Keating, till he burnt his feet on a roasting hot Uisce cover set into the footpath.

'Me brudder Tommy and that crowd from Glenconnor are going down the Green after dinner,' Jimmy announced.

Peadar was immediately mad to go with them. 'Jesus, Mary and Joseph, I'm meltin',' he said. 'Sure why don' we go down the Green wid d'lads? T'will be some craic. Will ye go, Jimmy?'

'I will,' said Jimmy.

'Will ye go, Finbarr?'

'Ah, I might...' Finbarr weighed his options, fingering the brown scapular round his neck that had freed itself from under his T-shirt. Saying he would ask his mother or that he would not be allowed would be the easy way out, but such damage to his status would take a serious number of goals, points and solo runs to repair. On the other hand it would be worse to go and hang back on the bank for fear of the water and get called chicken.

Maybe he should cop on to himself and go into the river with the others. He thought he could bear slipping down into the soft brown pull of the river current and feeling the soft mud between his toes and the weeds wrapping round his legs, and it would be a way of cooling off certainly, but what if he got out of his depth? He could not swim. Worst of all, if he went to the Green and got in the water, would they all start jumping off the Frosty Kennedy bridge and expect him to join in?

As he was debating these points to himself, Marion appeared round the corner waving urgently, like, as Finbarr said to himself later, 'an angel of God'. Finbarr had never been so pleased to see her.

'Ye're to come up home right now,' she panted, 'Aunt Julia is after arriving and she wants ye.'

'Ah, lads,' groaned Finbarr to Jimmy and Peadar, though inside his heart was singing. 'Jeez, I'm sorry lads, but I've to go in and see me aunt. Ye go on wid'out me and I'll get down to ye later if I can.'

He caught up with Marion and played it cool. 'Wha's with Aunt Julia tha' she wants to see me?' he grumbled.

'Ye're goin' on a holiday if ye want,' was Marion's surprising reply. 'She's invited ye down to Waterford till next Monday. Uncle Paddy's after hurtin' his foot and he wants help in the bar. She says he'll pay ye an' all.'

Finbarr brightened. He couldn't believe his luck. If he went to Waterford he would miss the whole ordeal of the river - the splashing, the shouts, the messing, the fear of being pulled under by some fool acting the maggot. It had happened to him once in the pool and he had got an awful fright and never gone back, which was why he had never learnt to swim.

The weatherman had said that the big 'H' was moving on to smother London by next Monday. Once the weather broke it would be safe for Finbarr to come home and pick up his usual pursuits, with solid concrete under his feet and his lungs filled with nothing but fresh air flavoured with turf smoke and the tang from the abattoir nearby.

So it was that an hour and a half later Finbarr was cooling down by sticking his head out of the front window of Aunt Julia's Fiat, heading down the N24 to Waterford. He wound up the window going past the Miloko factory however, and Aunt Julia told him the dreadful smell was nothing to do with chocolate crumb being made at the factory at all, and everything to do with the pig farm just behind it.

In Piltown they stopped at John Tobin's shop and Aunt Julia had a chat and bought two cones with flakes in. As they rolled past the wide brown stretch of the river at Fiddown, Finbarr laughed to himself. His troubles with the river were far away behind him, thirty miles upstream in Clonmel.

'Nearly there,' said Aunt Julia too soon, just before they got caught at the level crossing by the reed beds going into the city. The boat-train headed for Rosslare passed them and next thing they were swinging past

Sally Park with a fine view of the Redmond Bridge that crossed the Suir to Waterford Quay. Opposite them the shops, offices, pubs and guest houses were painted in a striking array of colours stretching down to Reginald's Tower on their left.

Finbarr was interested in the bridge. It broke in half and had two sides that lifted up to let big ships go through. His aunt was telling him what times he could expect to see the bridge being raised when his eye was caught by a row of black flags.

The flags did not look as though they were meant to be there. They hung from the first of two steel gantries that made square arches over the pedestrians and traffic on the bridge. They looked like the flags that he sometimes got to wave at matches, white for a point, green for a goal, but these were sombre black. They were attached to little sticks of timber, each with a length of black cloth suspended from it that fluttered in the coastal breeze.

'Wha' are those flags up there for?' he asked, staring. He counted them. There were eight.

'Ye'd better ask your uncle,' replied Aunt Julia, uncharacteristically tight-lipped. Next thing she dropped Finbarr off outside his uncle's lounge bar and went to 'take round the car'. Townsfolk stabled their cars in a lock-up shed as faithfully as country people might stable a horse or a jennet.

Finbarr stood on the pavement with his sports bag gripped in his hand, looking up at the pub. The pillars either side of the door and the hand-lettered sign above the single large window were freshly painted in green and cream. In a three-sided space behind the window, in front of a screen of tongue-and-groove panelling topped with panels of frosted glass, there stood a collection of dusty old bottles. The labels were so faded that some were unreadable, but Finbarr could make out 'Guinness', 'Harp' and 'Paddy – Light Irish Whiskey.' He felt proud when he recognised an old-style Bulmer's cider bottle. Jimmy's father worked at the factory in Clonmel where it was made. In the autumn there was a smell of apples around Dowd's Lane and a few opportunistic boys hanging around trying to rob a few, just for the craic.

Finbarr was delighted by the set-up in Waterford. Aunt Julia's youngest son was away on an F.C.A. camp, so Finbarr had a bedroom to himself. It faced towards the river and he had a view of some of the rock face above Sally Park. At a high flat spot, visible from all over town, graffiti spelt out 'H block' in letters with paint drips running from them.

Finbarr did his Uncle Paddy's jobs with enthusiasm. He fetched boxes of bottles up from the cellar and rolled beer barrels outside and stacked them in the mornings. He washed bottles and glasses and sorted out the returns. He felt particularly grand if a local child came in with a big returnable mineral bottle and handed it over. Finbarr had instructions to strike the red bar on the till in this situation and give the child a ten pence piece. Meanwhile Uncle Paddy sat on one of the faux-leather seats under photographs of greyhounds, racehorses and the All-Ireland winning Waterford team of 1948, his injured foot in its plaster-cast stuck out in front of him, raging at the contents of the Irish Independent.

When the bar was quiet during the day Finbarr went out to see the lifting of the Bridge. He looked down at the docks and saw the cranes lifting and stacking the huge shipping containers. After tea with Aunt Julia in the kitchen it was time to go through into the bar and help collect glasses.

By now the air was hazy with cigarette smoke and rich with the mingled smells of whiskey and porter. Men's deep voices roared and laughed. They told jokes and argued about sport, criticised referees, lambasted players and cursed the government. Everyone was on the look-out for a good thing at the racecourse too, and the names of horses rang out like a litany: Blue Wind, Woodstream, Shergar, King's Lake.

Finbarr kept thinking of what Jimmy and Peadar would say if they could see him now. It seemed like a great step up from kids' games on the street to the world of men to be here in the bar every night, even if he was just collecting the empty beer glasses with white froth stuck to their sides. The lads would be mad with envy. He was avoiding the short-lived summer madness around swimming in the Suir and to cap it all, was also earning a whole pound note a day from his uncle. He could hardly get over his luck.

Later in the night when people had had a few jars, someone started up on the squeeze-box and another fella on the guitar. The songs in Uncle Paddy's bar seemed to follow a regular programme. They were mostly folk and rebel songs, some of which Finbarr knew, but 'The Men Behind the Wire' was new to him. It was very popular in Uncle Paddy's bar however. On Saturday night the lock-in went on till three in the morning though regretfully Finbarr had to do as his aunt told him and go up to bed at half past midnight.

The atmosphere amongst Uncle Paddy's regular clientele and companions seemed different next evening though. Finbarr wondered at the grave and angry faces, till Uncle Paddy put a black bow on the door. A hunger-striker had died in the Maze prison in the North and the talk on the high stools was muted and serious.

'Nine,' Uncle Paddy was saying, 'he's the ninth. Nine more martyrs for poor auld Ireland.' His friends Mr. O'Dea and the man from the shop opposite agreed sadly. Uncle Paddy had a rule not to drink in his own pub but on this occasion he set his rule aside and poured himself a slow pint. While the froth on the Guinness was settling he helped himself to a Powers with a splash of red lemonade from the big bottle on the bar counter. Mr. O'Dea and the shopkeeper pushed forward their glasses and said, 'Same again.'

The talk in the pub that night was like the buzzing of angry hornets. The horses, hurlers and jokes had vacated the smoke between the frosted glass at the window and the gleam of the polished bar. It was all about the North.

Finbarr did not know much about politics other than what he had picked up at home. His mother always said that Ireland couldn't afford the North. When they watched the news on the 12th of July his father tut-tutted and said both sides should 'cop on'. In Uncle Paddy's bar though, it was clear that Bobby Sands, M.P. was a hero. The singing grew noisy, then maudlin. Men of all ages took turns to sing solos. Uncle Paddy sang 'Only our rivers run free' and grew emotional.

'Finbarr,' he said, 'all our war songs are happy and our love songs are sad. Isn't that right, boy?'

Finbarr nodded cautiously and said he supposed so. He did not feel altogether comfortable in the bar that night. It was as though the current of the stream of conversation had changed and he had been swept out of his depth. Just then Aunt Julia put her head round the door to call Finbarr to bed. Finbarr put down the linen cloth he was holding in relief, but Uncle Paddy, red-faced and louder than usual, objected.

'Go 'way to bed yourself, Julia. The young fella'll come when he's good and ready, isn't that right, Finbarr? Go on and get a bottle of Cidona for yourself and sit down here and have a little drink with me and the lads.'

Avoiding Aunt Julia's eye, Finbarr did as his Uncle said. When he was sitting down his Uncle clumsily sloshed half his whiskey into Finbarr's glass.

'Sure what's wrong with the women anyway,' he demanded. 'Always fussing and complaining. Go way outta that with the hitting the leaba. Ye'd rather come on a little adventure with me and the lads, hey?'

The whiskey clawed at the back of Finbarr's throat and took his breath away but he felt invincible after the first sip. 'Yeah,' he said, feeling the after-burn of the whiskey sting in his mouth and nose, 'I would o'course.' He reached for his glass again.

Time seemed to take on a peculiar quality after that. At some point Finbarr realised he was standing on the quay with two men but he was no longer sure whether he knew who they were or not. His Uncle was nowhere to be seen.

Finbarr's ears were no longer pounded by the sound of raucous singing. Instead he could hear the quiet lapping of water against the quay wall. The street lights were turned off as it was after midnight, but the piercing eye of a red traffic light illuminated the entrance to the bridge. Finbarr noticed one of the men was carrying a coil of rope.

'C'mon so,' said the rope-carrier.

'Where's Uncle Paddy?' Finbarr blurted out. The rush of the cold outside air hitting him was helping him think straighter.

'Isn't he inside in the bar waiting for you with a packet of Taytos and a hot whiskey when you get back,' said the other man smoothly. 'Sure he had to give this expedition a miss on account of the foot. 'Tis why we decided on someone a bit lighter this time.'

'If ye drop a horse down a thousand-yard mineshaft it splashes but a mouse just gets a little shock and runs away,' said the rope-carrier wisely.

They crossed the empty street, turned onto the great bridge and walked in silence under the first gantry and past the mid-line where the two halves of the bridge met. A triangular metal rampart sloped upwards on each side of them. Finbarr could see the temptation to climb up its gentle diagonal. From the top of it the lattice-work of blue-painted steel bars spanning the bridge could be reached quite easily by someone fit and strong.

It was this gantry that bore the eight black flags. Finbarr now knew they were commemorating the hunger strikers. He had learnt a lot in the last few days. It seemed odd that only three days ago he had passed under those flags and not known why they were there. He felt he had grown-up somehow.

The man with the rope was throwing it over the gantry and securing one end to the side of the bridge. He tested it with his weight. The softly-spoken man took a black flag from inside his jacket. He handed it to Finbarr, a length of rough wood with an expanse of black cotton furled tightly around it.

'You can use the rope to help you up the incline there, and then to hoist yourself onto the gantry. 'Tis just like a big climbing frame. See how the other flags are arranged? You go on up there and tie this one up just the same.'

Finbarr felt confused. He could not remember agreeing to go climbing on a bridge in the dark like this. The climb looked easy and he did not think he minded one way or the other about the flag really, but it was hard to be sure. He had never taken much notice of the Troubles. He didn't know what he thought.

Finbarr clambered onto the sloping metal rampart at the side of the bridge. The steel was icy cold and little bumps of rust dug into his hand. He took the slope at a stooping run and only needed to make the rope take his weight when he got near the top and had to make the transition onto the horizontal overhead.

Once he made the mistake of looking down. The road swayed and danced beneath him and to his right was the perilous drop into the black abyss of the river. Finbarr closed his eyes and gripped the L-shaped steel bars of the gantry with both hands. For a moment he felt paralysed. He dare not let go of his hand-holds. He clung grimly to the bars ignoring the muttering of the men on the road several feet below.

Finbarr took a few deep breaths of river air and determined to focus only on his immediate surroundings, the criss-cross lattice of bars that supported him. He crawled and slithered across the gantry to the spot pointed out to him. The black flag was tucked down his T-shirt, with its end held securely in the waistband of his jeans.

Finbarr wedged himself into a space in the metal framework, wrapping each leg round a support and leaning his elbows across the bars so that his hands were free to fish twine out of his pocket. His hands seemed to be shaking as he secured the flag, obeying the hoarse whispers from below telling him to correct the angle to match the others.

When the flag was in position Finbarr unwound his legs and realised that while he had been concentrating on tying the flag, his legs had become stiff and cramped. Pins and needles shot through them as he started to crawl back over the gantry. Ahead of him he could not avoid seeing lights from moored ships and buildings glittering over the ever-changing surface of the water. Empty space seemed to pull at his feet so that instead of finding a safe foothold they were drawn off course towards the treacherous water beneath. He swayed and heard alarmed voices from the footpath.

'Aisy there, son. Have you the rope? Turn round and leave yourself down backaways. Aisy does it, that's the way. Good man yerself, Finbarr, that's great work.'

They pulled down the rope and set off back towards the city. The distant light of a slow-moving vehicle could be seen approaching up the quay.

'Jaysus, 'tis the guards!' exclaimed the rope-man.

'Walk normally,' instructed his companion. 'Don't speed up.' He touched Finbarr on the shoulder to get his attention. 'Finbarr, if they stop to speak to us you run for it back to your uncle's and go in round the back way, d'ye understand.'

A few moments later the two men started laughing as the tail-lights of the squad car receded over the bridge. Back in the pub Uncle Paddy was inclined to make much of Finbarr's exploits. He even hobbled over to the kettle himself to make the promised hot whiskey, but Finbarr felt dead-beat. He just wanted to go to bed.

'Go on so,' said Uncle Paddy genially. 'And mind now, not a word about tonight to your aunt.'

'Best say nothing to anyone,' said the man with the soft voice, lighting a cigarette and shaking out the match.

Next day was Monday. The heat wave had subsided and there was even a shower of rain. Aunt Julia insisted on making the trip to Clonmel as soon as Finbarr had helped with the delivery from the brewery. ''Tis as well he gets on home,' she said repressively to her husband, picking up her car keys when Uncle Paddy protested. 'About time we saw some Johnny-Jump-Up from you and that auld foot. Or you could pay someone a proper wage instead of taking advantage of my sister's child.'

Finbarr shut his eyes going over the Redmond Bridge. He didn't know whether it had been the whiskey or the climb, or the sense of being drawn into some shadowy secret that he barely understood, but he just wanted to get home and forget about it now.

He fingered the pound notes in his pocket. He would treat Jimmy and Peadar to chips from Miss

Ellie's. If there was a match later they'd go down to the field. If there wasn't, he didn't much fancy climbing over the wall today, but there was always the street and walking to Walsh's under the orange glow of the street lamps for chocolate or a can.

Maybe...Finbarr had a bright idea that made him feel an unusual glow of warmth inside... maybe he'd buy his mother a bag of Emerald toffees. She liked those. In fact, maybe he'd get the toffees, leave the chips till tomorrow and just go in early and watch the news with the family. It would be grand to just get back to normal, with one exception.

He thought he had left the river behind in Clonmel but it had only been twice as wide and terrible in Waterford. So after the toffees and chips he decided he would save the rest of his money for going to the pool. This time, whatever it took, Finbarr was finally going to learn to swim.

Caitlín

Caitlín lived in a small white cottage tucked into a fold of the Comeragh mountains. Her house was flanked by two lines of barns and byres and hemmed in by a low stone wall in front. Three sash windows and a half-door looked out from the cottage onto a square yard. The roof of the house was of grey slate and at both ends a white stone chimney rose out of it. Winter or summer, from early morn till midnight, smoke could be seen rising from those chimneys out over the forest, above the mountains and far away.

The twisting boreen outside Caitlín's wall rambled away to the road that crossed the Comeraghs between Clonmel and Ballymac. Caitlín could sit on her rock in the yard, a chunk of the mountain said to have been thrown there by a giant, for a whole day without seeing a single car, a single horse, a single person. Along that whole boreen there were only two deserted cottages and Caitlín's house, which still breathed fresh air through the half-door and puffed out turf smoke from the chimneys.

Mammy was plump and tended to be breathless. She wore long tartan skirts with winceyette petticoats to keep out the mountain wind. Her busy feet bustled here and there in furry slippers inside the house and Wellington boots outside in the yard. Pappy was small but strong, in his grey pants and jacket and with his flat peaked cap pulled low over his eyes. Gerry, Sylvie and Niall were Caitlín's brothers. They were all tall like Mammy and strong like Pappy. Gerry was the oldest and he was good-tempered. Brother Sylvie was the opposite for he tended to be cross. Niall, the youngest of the three, was a cheerful soul who liked to tease.

One day in August Caitlín was eating her breakfast of cornflakes with milk from Spot the cow, when she noticed the big space beside the fire where the supply of turf should be. Wasn't it only yesterday that she had poked her head inside the turf shed and thought how bare it was? Of course, Pappy said nearly every evening at tea that next day he would finally give some time to the bog, but every day some more pressing job prevented him going.

Caitlín wandered over to the big Stanley range. The day was sunny but Mammy had lighted it early as usual, to heat the water for washing. The neglected gas stove stood unnoticed in the corner. Mammy liked to cook on the range when she had it hot anyway, and not be wasting money and chasing in and out to the village for gas bottle refills.

Caitlín basked in the warmth of the stove and rubbed her toe over the turf dust on the floor, considering the problem. Gerry and Sylvie had work with other farmers and had already gone bumping off down the boreen, sandwiched together on the seat of the little red moped. Pappy and Niall had some important job on their own land to attend to.

Caitlín, glancing round the table, resolved to go up to the bog herself to fetch some turf. One evening in July Pappy had taken her there in the ancient Morris minor, so she knew just where their turf was. Caitlín had helped mark the place by writing in felt-tip on lengths of scrap timber stuck into the ground.

As for going alone to the bog, she would tell no-one, for they would be sure to forbid it. They would probably say it was too hard for a girl, or dangerous. Mammy always insisted she should concentrate on her studying and that there was no future on the land for hill farmers anyway.

Caitlín knew it was not just because she was a girl though, but because she was such a pale, sickly girl. She had huge greenish-grey eyes peering out of a thin white face. Her legs and arms were skinny and white and her peaked face was crowned with a bird's nest of wispy hair. Caitlín did not think she was as delicate as they all supposed but still Mammy fussed about keeping her warm and loading her plate up with green vegetables. Well today she would show them what a girl could do!

So directly after she had helped do the wash-up she crept out to the stable and fetched her bike. It had a large basket in front of the handlebars but to push it all the way to the bog for the amount of turf that would hold would be madness. Caitlín poked around amongst the old junk stored here and her eye fell on a cart made from the bottom half of a tea chest and the base of a pram. Her brothers had made it and tried to hitch it, unsuccessfully, to a goat. Then they had tried driving it down hills but the cart had turned out to be unstable and impossible to steer. One visit to the bonesetter later to attend to Gerry's right arm they had all been forbidden to take it out of the yard.

That had been years ago, however. Caitlín was sure that attaching it to the back of her bike and taking it to the bog to benefit everyone was not a crime. She searched out some lengths of baling twine and various bits of leather harness left over from a long-forgotten donkey, and happily worked away till her handiwork passed the test. When she pushed the bike the cart obligingly followed behind without wobbling too much or bumping the back mudguard.

Out through the gate crept Caitlín with her contraption. She walked with it down the shady boreen to where a rough track led upwards to the bog. The tarmac road in the other direction offered a smoother surface but it twisted and turned, adding extra miles, and was mostly too steep to cycle anyway. Straight across the hillside would be shorter and, she thought, more fun.

Up on the hill there was nobody to see her but sheep with different coloured paint splodges on them. Some bore Pappy's mark. Those with different marks belonged to friends and neighbours. Caitlín pushed her bike and its trundling cart onwards up the stony track. It was a sunny morning and sometimes she came across little groups of sheep lying on the stones, which were warm from the sun. When the sheep heard Caitlín they hurried up onto stick-like legs and nimbly bounded away.

At last she came to a place level enough to cycle. The ride was slow and jerky and she concentrated on navigating safely between the dusty grey stones, ruts and pot-holes. Her hair waved behind her but before her was the wide expanse of bog and heather reaching to the sky. The ridge of the Seven Sisters cradled the bog to her right. The peaks looked close, as if she could reach the top and see over the other side in five minutes, but the distance was deceptive. Even from where she was it would be a long hard climb to the top.

Caitlín stopped for a rest. The bog was a patchwork of emerald and corn-coloured grasses, dotted with fluffy white tufts of bog cotton blowing in the wind. A stark ribbon of black marked the cutaway, where sleans had sliced down into the turf bank.

Above the black earth mosses and grass grew like a coat of green hair. At the foot of the cutaway a deep ditch held black water.

Between Caitlín and the cutaway the grass was rough and sods of turf had been laid out to dry. Mostly the sods were propped up against each other like little castles, lines and lines of them, stretching impressively to the blue horizon. Patches of trampled grass marked places where some families had already saved their turf and carried it away in trailers and vans and the boots of cars.

When she had looked a long while at the undulating reaches of the bog and the serrated outline of the mountain ridge, Caitlín recalled her mission to mind. She was there, she told herself sternly, to fetch turf, not to stare around like she had never seen a bog before. She set off once more, leaning over the handlebars to push the bike and hearing the squeak of a wheel and the rumble of the cart over the rough ground. From above her head there came a piping and twittering of skylarks.

Caitlín thought of all the warnings she had ever been given about the danger of bogs. The inviting mounds that looked like cushions of soft green velvet were places where the ground shook if you jumped up and down. The rushes hid sly soft marshes that could pull you down, or cunning pot-holes that would soak your feet. In the puddly parts grew sundews, with tiny leaves bejewelled with sticky drops atop stiff pink hairs. They would not harm a human but Pappy said those cunning little leaves were designed to kill flies and midges.

At last Caitlín thought she recognised the right place. She propped the bike up on its metal prong and bent down to examine the wooden posts stuck into the ground. The ground here was dry and firm with sunny yellow flowers and bells of eyebright dappling the sheep-bitten grass. She was glad she had marked their posts clearly, with big purple letters. Now she knew she was in the right place but as she looked out over the cut turf, her face fell in dismay.

Where were all the tidy stooks Pappy and the boys had made? The pieces of turf should be arranged in little castles, four stout ones propped against each other and crowned with a cap of smaller raggedy ones. Some of Pappy's stooks were still standing but in many places the sods of turf lay scattered about on the ground. Every night they would absorb the dew from the ground and all the good work of the sun and the drying wind would be undone.

Sure enough, when Caitlín picked up one of the brown bars of turf, its underside was dark, wet and spongy. Only the top was hardened in light brown ridges, dry and sharp to the touch. Too late Caitlín remembered Mammy warning her that turf would 'cut the hands offa ya'. She wished she had remembered to bring gloves.

Caitlín started to foot the turf, re-building the stooks. Her mission now was far more than just fetching a sack or two of fuel to surprise Mammy. Now she, Caitlín, at this late stage in the summer, must single-handedly save the turf.

It was fun at first, exercising her skill. She had to choose two sods that were evenly matched in size and place them just right so that they leaned against each other and stayed standing upright. Next two more sods were laid opposite each other, against the first two. All four had their damp sides outermost so the wind would whip past them and the sun would warm them, drawing away the moisture and leaving them hard and burnable. On top of her four supports, lifted even higher to the face of the sun and caress of the mountain breeze, went any awkward lumps, too small or misshapen to use as pillars.

Half a row on however Caitlín straightened up and noticed that her back was stiff. It was exhilarating to be alone on the wide bog, on top of the world it seemed, but bending and choosing and lifting and arranging the turf was making her back hurt and her hands sore. She wondered who had vandalised their stooks, giving her all this extra labour. Maybe she would take a walk to the end of this line just to see how long it really was. It seemed to go on forever but it must surely end somewhere.

Three sheep stared at her and ran away as she approached. Two of them barged through a few stooks as they went, scattering the sods. The other tried to jump and sent another little turf castle crashing to the ground. 'G'way, you villains!' cried Caitlín, waving her arms at them, and they streamed away towards the higher ground. So now she knew who the vandals were.

Caitlín worked on, re-ordering the scattered ranks, rebuilding the collapsed towers. As she worked she started humming a tune. It was 'The Foggy Dew,' her brother Niall's favourite song. Caitlín knew every word from hearing him roaring it as he went about his work. Then she sang a skipping song that Mammy had taught her:

'Oh, she is handsome, she is pretty,

She is the belle of Dublin city.

She is a-courtin' one, two, three,

Pray will you tell me, who is she?'

That reminded her of playing skipping games with her friends back at National School, but they were all in first year now and liked pop music better. Adam Ant was their favourite.

'Stand and deliver! Whoo! Whoo!' whooped Caitlín. She enjoyed singing that line to the recalcitrant bars of turf that fell as soon as she tried to set them balancing each other. Some were so awkward she gave up on them. They were too big and soggy and had absorbed too much moisture to stand properly. She propped the bad ones up against each other as well as she could in bigger groups, hoping the wind would still find its way around them somehow.

After a long time that seemed short since she was so engrossed in what she was doing, all the lines were done. Caitlín suddenly wondered what time it was. Time seemed to stand still up here on the bog but back at home Mammy would be boiling cabbage in the water the bacon had cooked in. As one o'clock approached she would be making a white sauce to go with it, and sliding the bubbling pot of Dungarvan queens to the cooler end of the range.

Caitlín began to panic. Into the cart she threw the driest sods she could find, the ones that weighed the lightest in her hand, from stooks that had been left standing and not been mown down by clumsy sheep. When the pram-cart was full and she tried to push her bike it was too heavy to move. Frustrated, she had to waste time taking some sods out and setting them upright once again. At last she mounted the bike and started off across the stony track with her harvest.

With the heavy cart behind it the bike wobbled violently this way and that. For a few minutes her imagination pictured what might happen if she fell off and got injured, trapped under the bike, with her precious cargo upturned on the heather. No one knew where to come looking for her. How long would she last without a drink of water in the brilliant sunshine? Would a sudden mountain mist come down and chill her? Would they find her before night? These melodramatic thoughts gave way to what Mammy would have to say about another £25 for a visit to the doctor, and she stood up on the pedals and pressed harder, steering a careful straight course with the weight of turf clunking after her.

As the path began to tilt downwards Caitlín dismounted and continued on foot. The purple-coloured shale on the path was slippery. If she placed her foot carelessly she could slide on an avalanche of sharp stones. The weight of the cart pushed the bike forward but Caitlín had to hold it back and tread carefully. The backs of her legs ached.

It was only when she had finally descended into the shade of the boreen that Caitlín noticed with a painful stab just how hungry she was. She had never been so hungry in all her life. She was so hungry that she felt light-headed and she wondered if, now so close, she would ever reach home on her shaking legs. If she did make it back and it wasn't time for dinner yet, would Mammy allow her a biscuit to save her life?

Caitlín stopped seeing the leaves above her and her dirty hands clutching the handlebars of the bike. In her mind's eye she pictured only the big red and white biscuit barrel. Were there Kimberleys left? She hoped there were Kimberleys. They were her favourites. Then she imagined biting into the sweet red jam and soft mallow of a Mikado, and she wished they were there too. Or Bourbons, sometimes Mammy bought those, or even the plain Marie biscuits, anything really. For the first time in her life Caitlín believed that she might actually be starving.

When she reached the front gate Mammy was going back into the house with the empty washing basket in her arms. The line was propped up on its long pole and shirts and vests were flapping in the breeze.

'Well,' she said, turning round at the sound of the gate, 'and where were ye gone to all mornin'?'

'Up at the bog,' replied Caitlín truthfully, 'Oh Mammy, is the dinner ready? I'm nearly collapsed with the hunger!'

'Lord save us, it is, girl!' exclaimed Mammy. 'Come in and take a glass of milk while you're waiting for Pappy. He's just washing his hands.'

Caitlín steadied her bike and cart against the wall of the stable and entered the house with two hard-earned sods of turf in her hands. It was dark after the brightness of the summer's day outside, so at first she could hardly see what was on the big kitchen table, but there was no mistaking the smell of boiled bacon and cabbage. Her insides curled with hunger and her mouth watered in anticipation. She dumped the turf on top of some ash blocks, headed for the table and got sent to the sink to wash her hands. The boys were already seated.

'Jeepers, Caitlín, what happened ye?' exclaimed Niall as Caitlín flopped heavily into her chair.

'I've been getting in the turf,' said Caitlín proudly, waving a hand towards her contribution by the hearth, but her eyes were fixed on the table. There was a slab of creamery butter in the butter dish and milk in the blue-and-white-striped jug. There were the little matching salt and pepper pots and the bottles of red and brown sauce. The spuds were already piled high in a Pyrex dish, their skins cracked and peeling away from them, fringed with a fuzz of burst potato. Pappy sat down and speared one with his fork and started peeling it onto a small plate.

'Balls of flour!' he said with relish. He said that nearly every day and they all agreed. He skilfully slipped the skin of his potato away using his knife and thumb. 'What's that you said you were at, Caitlín?'

Caitlín reached for a potato and without ever peeling it, or putting milk or salt or butter on it, she took a huge bite of it, skin and all. 'Gettin' in the turf,' she mumbled through that glorious mouthful of soft hot potato.

All round the table there was laughter. Pappy chuckled, Niall guffawed and Sylvie brayed, but Caitlín hardly registered any of it. Mammy had put her dinner plate down before her and there for her joyful eye to behold were three thick slices of ham, a mound of green and white cabbage and a beautiful glossy puddle of white sauce. Caitlín thought she had never seen anything so wonderful in all her life. The bog had been awe-inspiring with the skylarks singing and the bog cotton blowing, but it was nothing compared to the sight of that plate.

'Here,' said Mammy, sliding a peeled potato off her fork onto Caitlín's plate. 'The bog air, there's nothing would make a person so hungry.' Everyone around the table agreed in murmurs but nobody said much because they were all too busy eating. For a few minutes there was no sound but the scraping of cutlery and the end of the news on RTE 1 from the transistor radio on top of the fridge. Then, as her stomach began to feel contentedly full Caitlín began to explain about her mission. There was more laughter and jokes. Nobody seemed cross. Then Niall told stories meant to scare her, about bog bodies coming to life out of the ooze and wicked will'o'the wisps lighting false trails across the bog at night.

Pappy peeled Caitlín another potato and she mashed it up on the plate with milk, salt and butter and ate it slowly. Mammy got up to clear the plates and Pappy scraped his chair back on the floor and felt in his top pocket for his packet of Majors. There was a sort of lull, with the boys puffing on cigarettes and Mammy running the water in the sink to do the dishes. Caitlín moved over to the range and pulled the lever to riddle the ashes. That was her own turf in there now, warming her, and making the heavy black kettle purr.

Mammy was saying, 'Wasn't she great to foot the turf again? A little girl like that, and all you men neglecting your business on the bog for the summer. I suppose 'tis rhubarb tart you'll be wanting for your tea, and no consideration of whether there's anything to heat the oven to cook it in.'

Niall was still teasing. 'Ye'll make a right bog man yet, Caitlín. Won't she, Sylvie? Will we get the girl her own slean, d'ya think?'

'Sure isn't it a shame I let the donkey go,' joked Pappy, ash hanging from the end of his cigarette. 'Couldn't Caitlin be bringing us whole ass-rails of turf if she had more'n an auld bike to fetch it with!'

Caitlín however heard none of it. She had fallen back in the easy chair next to the range. A shifting mosaic of bog flowers and waving grasses had cleared from behind her closed eyelids. After all the morning's fresh air and exercise Caitlín, full of good food and a satisfying sense of achievement, was sound asleep.

'Ah, would you look?' whispered Mammy. 'She's worn out, the poor craytur!'

Pappy smiled. 'Mind you don't let on to her what Niall and myself were at this morning,' he said warningly.

'What were ye at, at all?' asked Mammy, wonderingly.

'Cutting the ash tree that fell in the winter storm,' said Niall, grinning. 'Is there room for Caitlín's turf in the shed at all, Da, or have we it filled to the very rafters already?'